The
Mike Pence
Coloring Book

Written & Illustrated
by
Darren Martin

With Creative Contributions by
Trevor Martin, Chuck Leonard, and Mike Pence.

For Mike,

Table Of Contents

Mikey Goes to Hollywood..................4
- Trump-Man & Robin
- The Vice President With The Dragon Tattoo
- Willy Wonka And The Bullshit Factory
- Silence Of The Mike
- Pencimus Maximus
- Jurassic Pence
- "300" Reasons Why Mike Pence is Tighter Than You!
- Guytanic
- The Lying King
- Some Like It Hot
- The Wizard Of Pence
- The Pence Is Right
- Home Alone 5: Mikey's Revenge
- Vice Rambo
- Sexual Predator

The Art of Mike..................20
- Mike Paints
- Mona Lisa-Pence
- The Scream Dream
- Gothic Pence
- Whistler's Mother Fucker
- Mike Warhol
- Goliath
- The Vice and The Kiss

Marketing with Mike..................29
- Little Miss Coppertone
- Pence Health
- I Wanna Be Like Mike
- Got Mike?
- I can't Believe It's Not Mike!
- Share A Coke With Mike
- From The Makers Of Oxy Clean
- Michael McDonald
- Marlboro Mike

Mike Around The World..................39
- Mayan Mike
- The Goddess Vishnu
- Mike Marley
- Hieroglyphic. Terrific.
- The Pyramid of Pence
- Chiquita Bananarama
- Pence In Paris
- Pope Pence
- Pensacola

Miscellaneous Mikes..................49
- The Vice In The Hat
- Trunk Pence
- Lil' Mike
- Holy Shit
- Six Pence None The Richer
- Mike The Fidget Spinner
- A Warm Bath
- Mascot Mike
- Wonder Womike
- The End

MIKEY GOES TO HOLLYWOOD

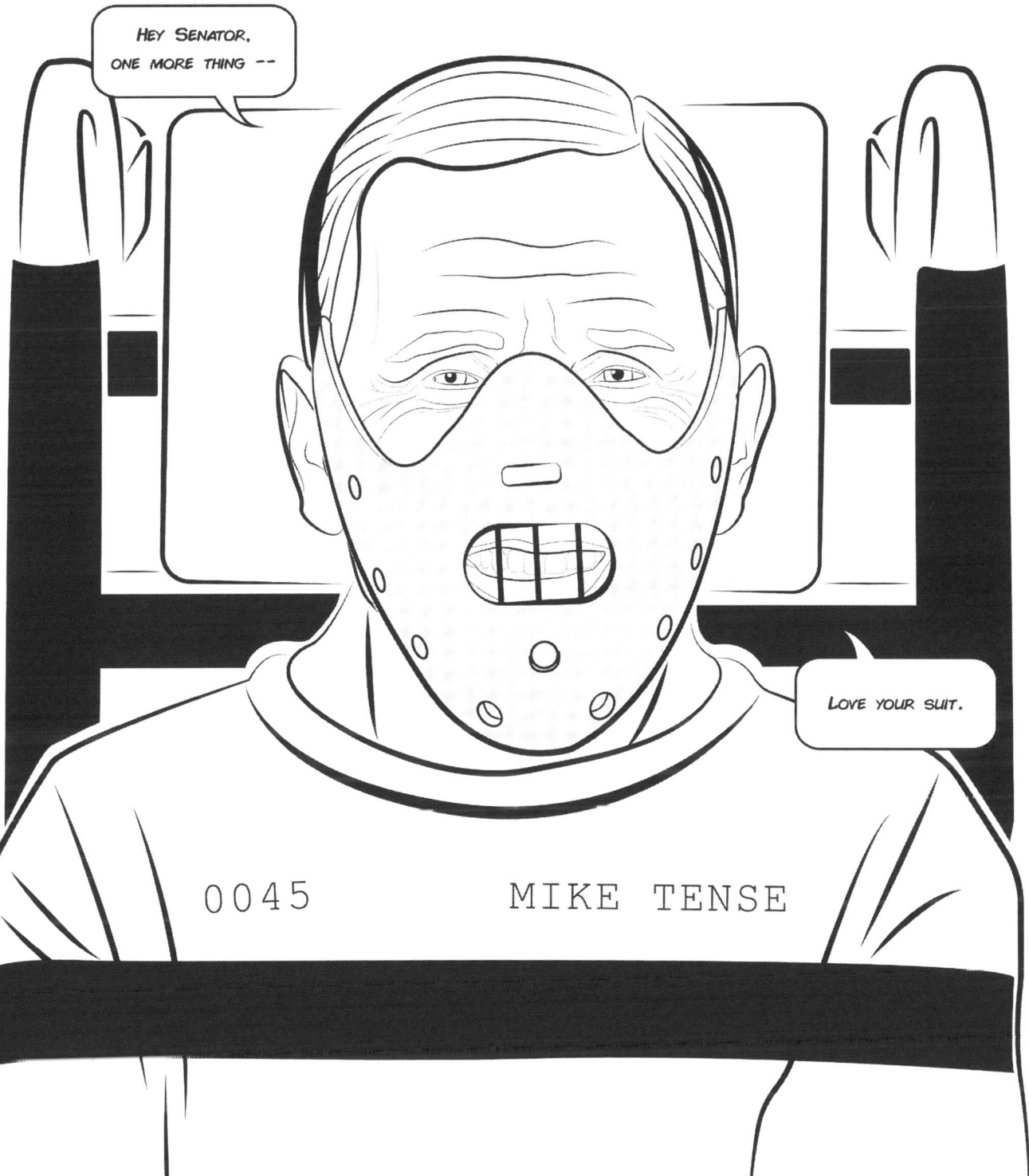

Sometimes 4 years... can feel like 65 million.

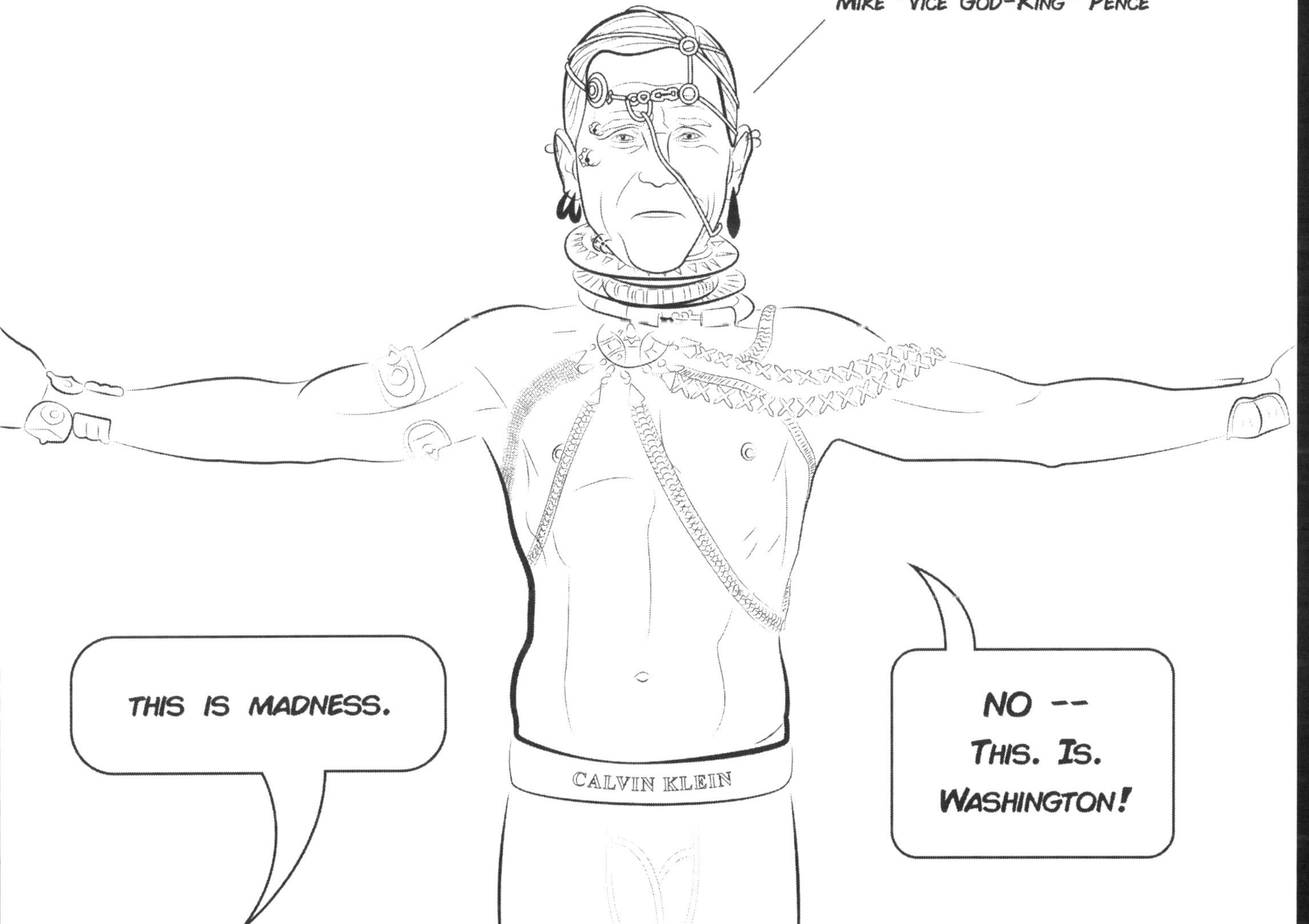

THE LYING KING

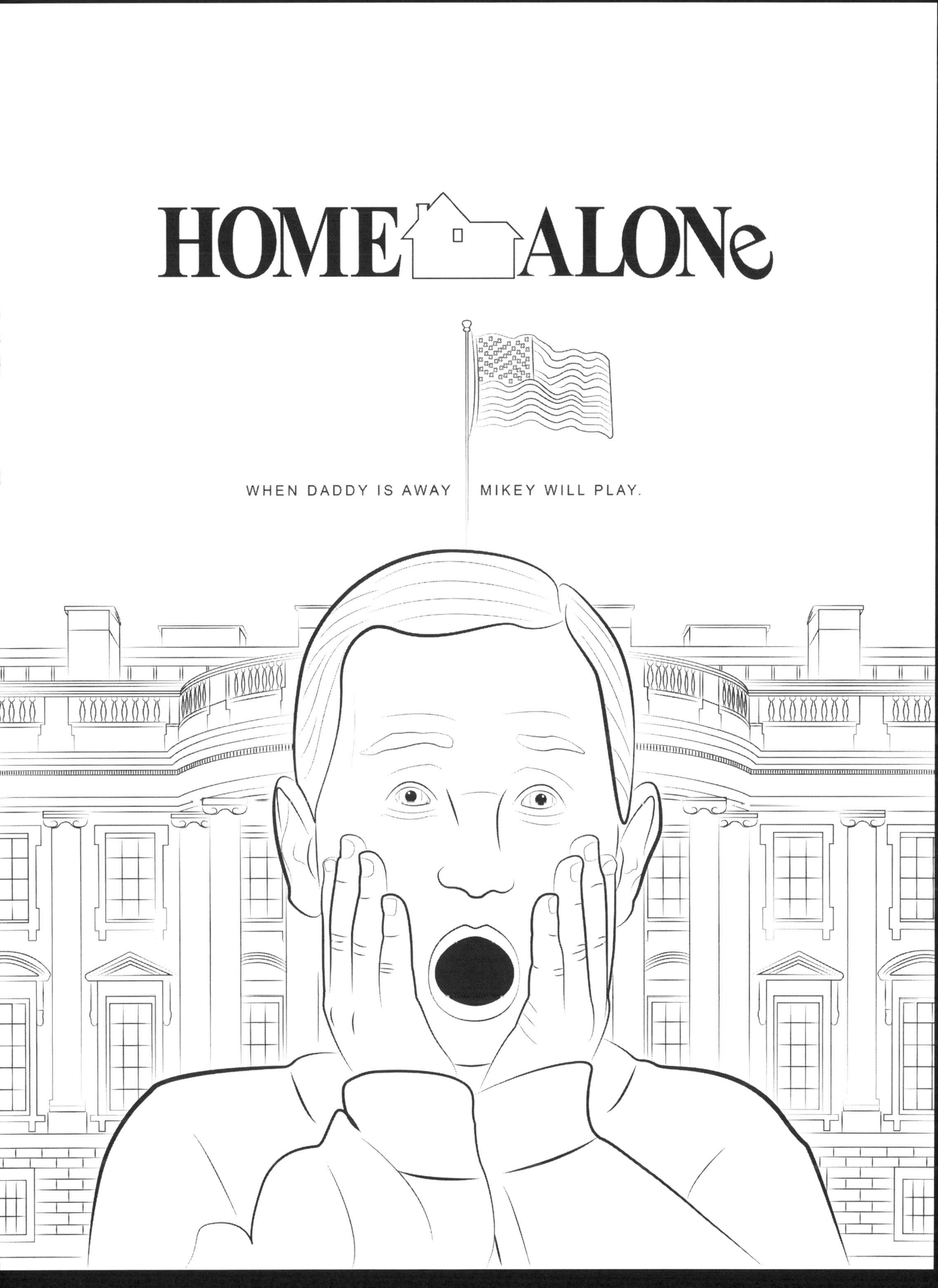

HOME 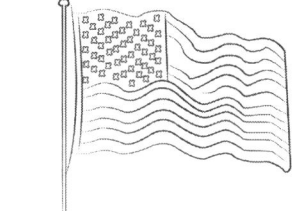 ALONe

WHEN DADDY IS AWAY   MIKEY WILL PLAY.

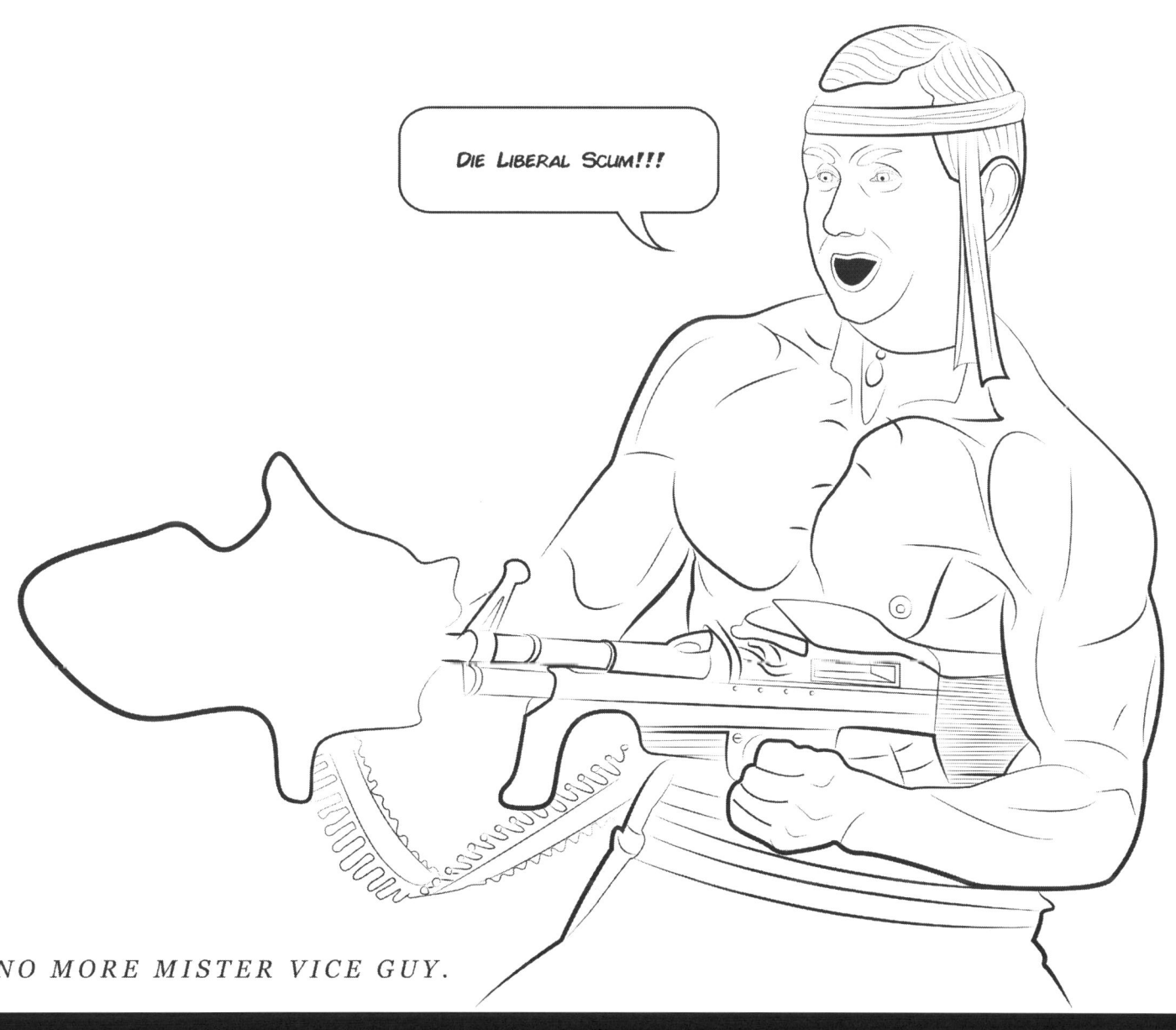

The Art of Mike

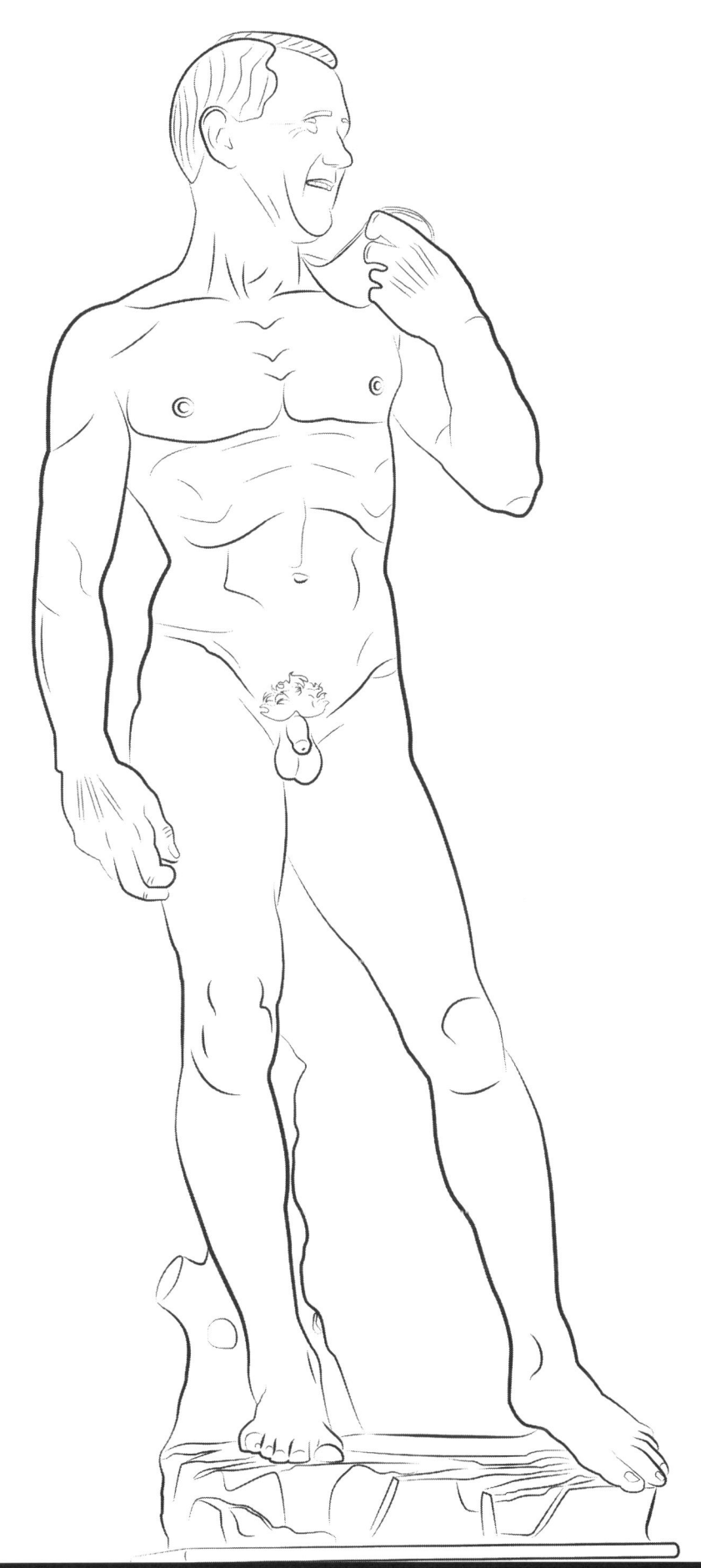

Marketing With Mike

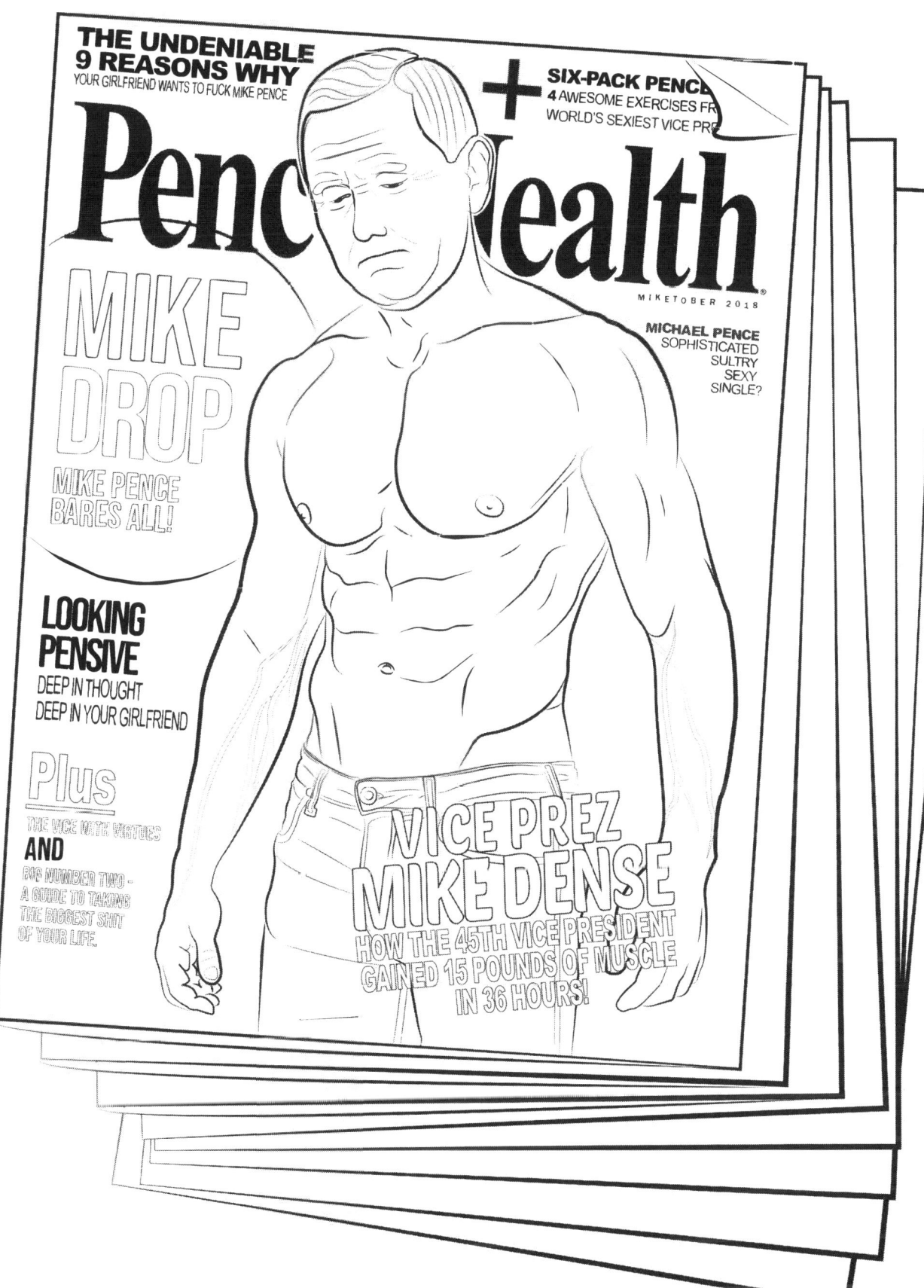

I WANNA BE LIKE MIKE.

Just Pence it.

Mike Around The World

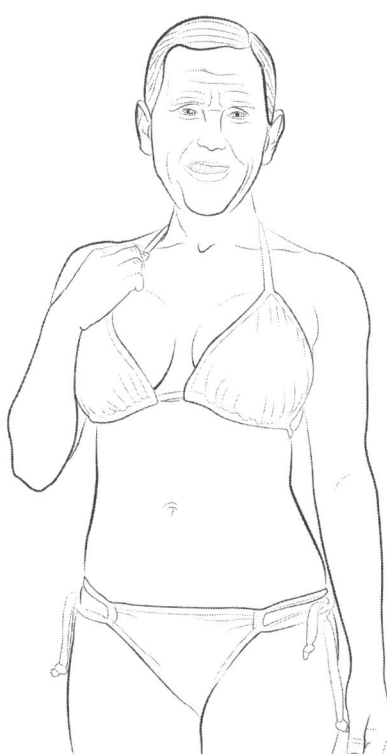

Miscellaneous Mikes

THE VICE IN THE HAT

Dr. Ben Carson

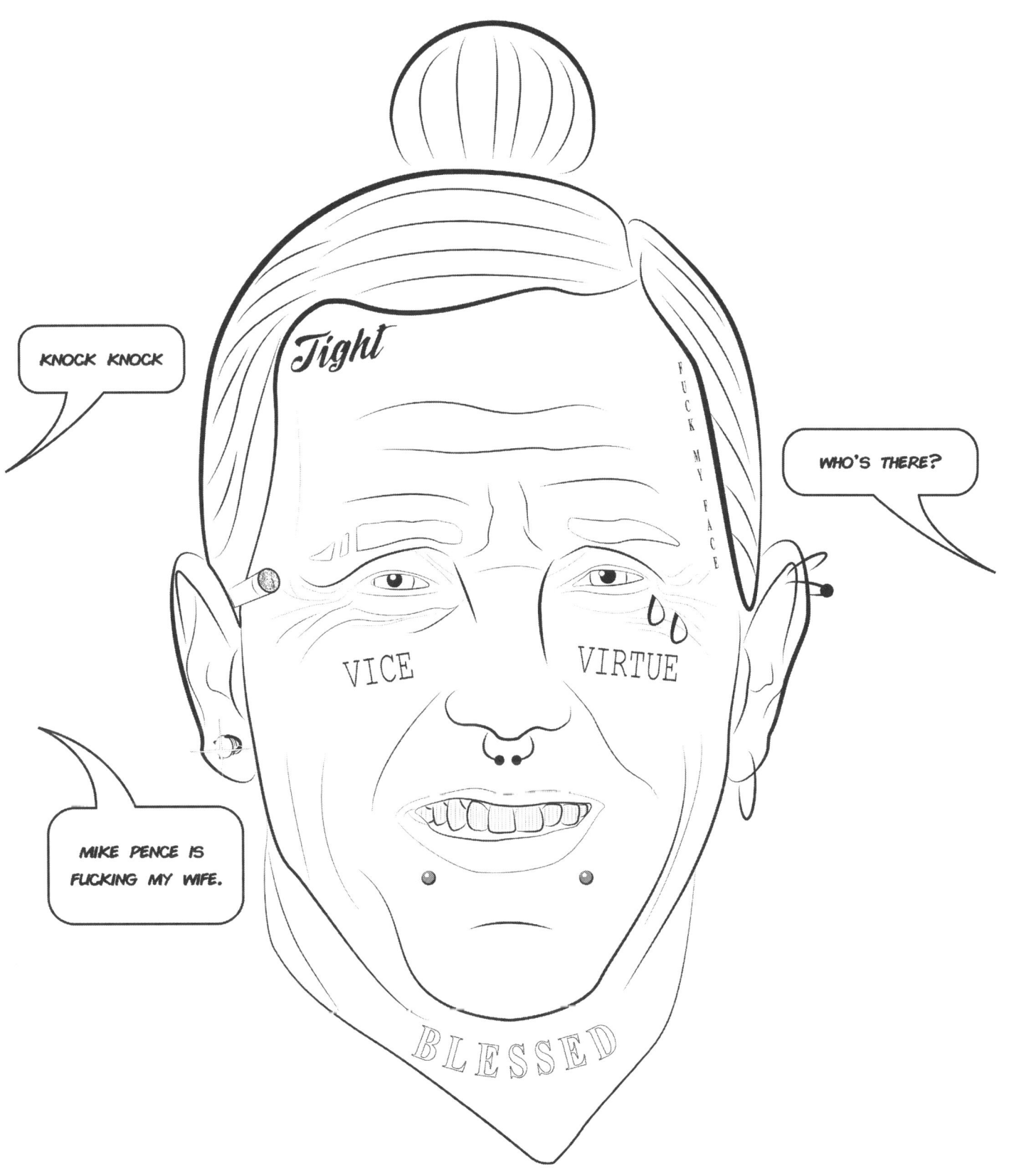

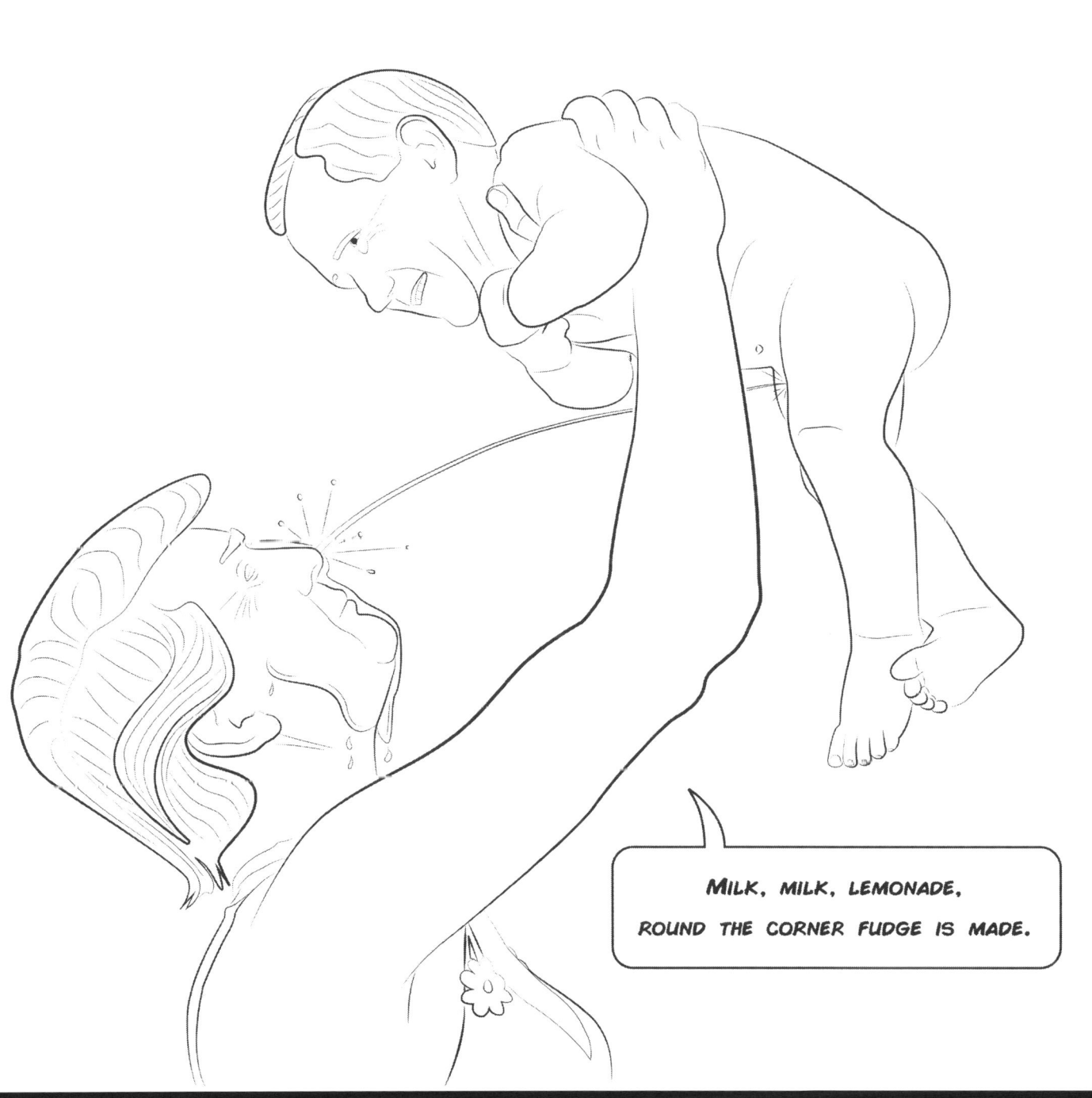

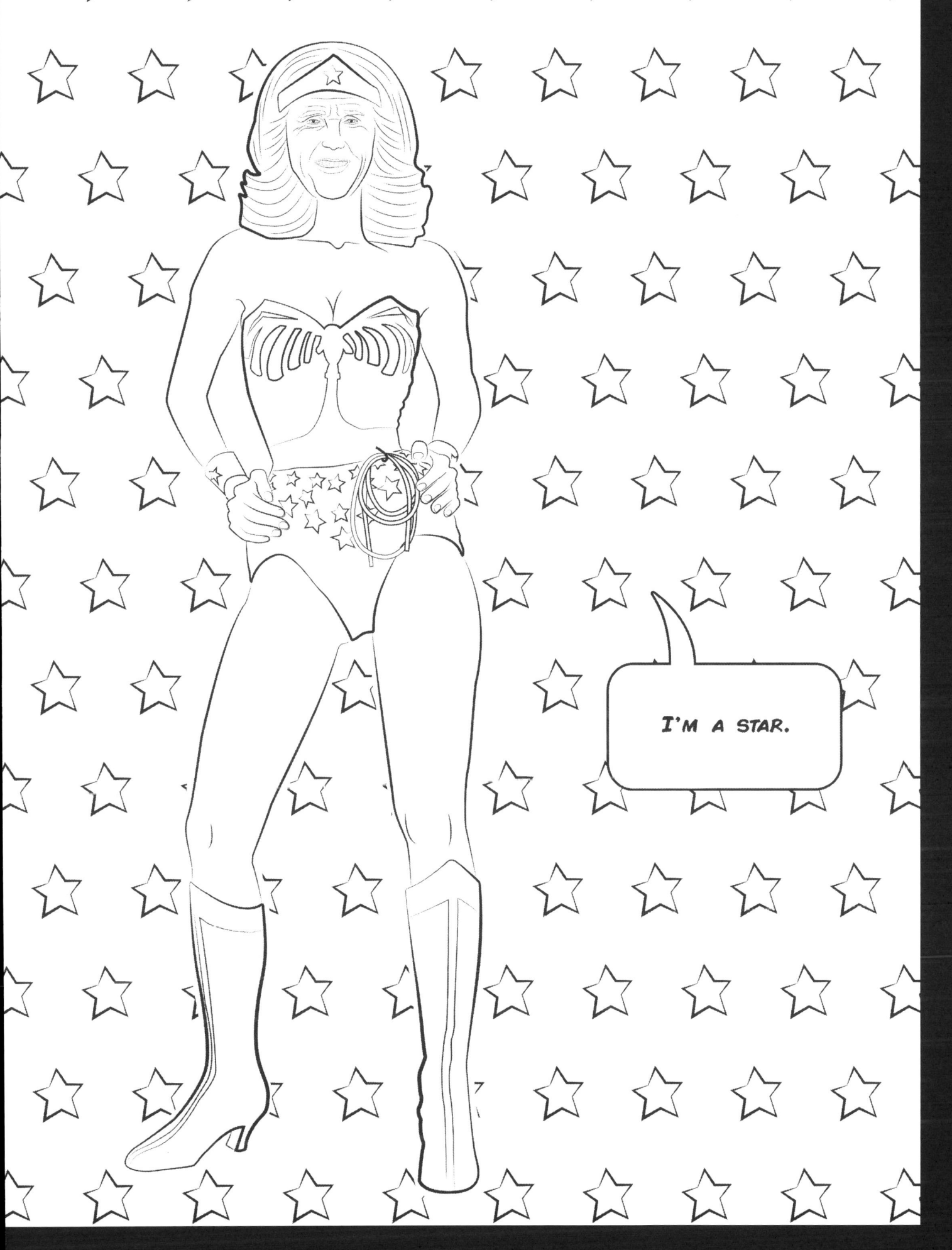

Special Thanks

Jake "The Snake" Flack

Matt "Big Chute" Keith

John Tuccillo Jr.

Robert "Wax Lord" Ruvalcaba

Joseph Ward

Mike Cummings

Grey "Little Monster" Robbins

Mike "Ice Box" McQuaid

The City of Pensacola

Coca-Cola

Trevor Martin

Chuck Leonard

Zeus The Dog

Mom

Dad

&

Mike Fucking Pence

About The Author

DARREN MARTIN IS AN ARTIST, COPYWRITER, AND COMEDIAN LIVING IN NORTH HOLLYWOOD, CA. WHEN HE'S NOT WORKING ON HIS STAND-UP COMEDY ROUTINE OR WRITING TAGLINES FOR FILM AND TELEVISION, HE'S PROBABLY MAKING SILLY ILLUSTRATIONS, SURFING AT EL PORTO, OR SPENDING TIME WITH HIS BEST FRIEND AND FAVORITE MALTESE-POODLE, ZEUS THE DOG. LIKE ANY TRUE VIRGO, DARREN ENJOYS LONG WALKS ON THE BEACH, THE FILMS OF PAUL GIAMATTI, REVERSE COWGIRL, AND INDICA. TO SEE MORE ILLUSTRATIONS OF MIKE PENCE AND HIS NEFARIOUS BAND OF CO-CONSPIRATORS, YOU CAN FOLLOW DARREN ON INSTAGRAM @DARRENILLUSTRATIONS.

THANKS AGAIN FOR PURCHASING *THE SUPER TIGHT MIKE PENCE ADULT COLORING BOOK* AND FOR DOING YOUR PART TO MAKE AMERICA GREAT AGAIN! WITH A LITTLE BIT OF HELP, AND WHOLE LOT OF PRAYER, WE WON'T HAVE TO PUT UP WITH 4 MORE YEARS OF THIS SHIT. AND BE SURE TO KEEP AN EYE OUT THIS SPRING FOR DARREN'S NEXT BOOK *THE CONSERVATIVE COLORING BOOK* FEATURING: MORE MIKE PENCE, TED CRUZ, DONALD TRUMP, BRET KAVANAUGH, SARAH SANDERS, KANYE WEST AND MUCH MORE!

Made in the USA
Monee, IL
20 December 2019